SLEEP ALL NIGHT!

HEALTHY SLEEPING HABITS

Mary Elizabeth Salzmann

Consulting Editor,
Diane Craig, M.A./ Reading Specialist

Sandcastle

An Imprint of Abdo Publishing
www.abdopublishing.com

www.abdopublishing.com

Published by Abdo Publishing, a division of ABDO, PO Box 398166, Minneapolis, Minnesota 55439.
Copyright © 2015 by Abdo Consulting Group, Inc. International copyrights reserved in all countries. No part of this book may be reproduced in any form without written permission from the publisher. SandCastle™ is a trademark and logo of Abdo Publishing.

Printed in the United States of America, North Mankato, Minnesota
102014
012015

THIS BOOK CONTAINS
RECYCLED MATERIALS

Editor: Alex Kuskowski
Content Developer: Nancy Tuminelly
Cover and Interior Design: Colleen Dolphin, Mighty Media, Inc.
Photo Credits: Shutterstock

Library of Congress Cataloging-in-Publication Data

Salzmann, Mary Elizabeth, 1968- author.

 Sleep all night! : healthy sleeping habits / Mary Elizabeth Salzmann.

     pages cm. -- (Healthy habits)

 Audience: Ages 4-9.

 ISBN 978-1-62403-531-9 (alk. paper)

1. Sleep--Physiological aspects--Juvenile literature. 2. Sleep--Juvenile literature. 3. Health--Juvenile literature. I. Title. II. Series: Salzmann, Mary Elizabeth, 1968- Healthy habits.

 QP425.S25 2015

 612.8'21083--dc23

                    2014023597

SandCastle™ Level: Transitional

SandCastle™ books are created by a team of professional educators, reading specialists, and content developers around five essential components—phonemic awareness, phonics, vocabulary, text comprehension, and fluency—to assist young readers as they develop reading skills and strategies and increase their general knowledge. All books are written, reviewed, and leveled for guided reading, early reading intervention, and Accelerated Reader® programs for use in shared, guided, and independent reading and writing activities to support a balanced approach to literacy instruction. The SandCastle™ series has four levels that correspond to early literacy development. The levels are provided to help teachers and parents select appropriate books for young readers.

EMERGING · BEGINNING · **TRANSITIONAL** · FLUENT

CONTENTS

WHAT IS A HEALTHY HABIT?

Getting enough sleep is a healthy **habit.**

You should sleep for at least 10 hours. That is a good night's sleep.

You will feel good when you wake up. You won't feel tired.

It can be hard to pay **attention** in school if you are tired.

You can feel too tired
to play if you don't
get enough sleep.

Jack reads in bed.
It helps him fall **asleep**.

Morgan drinks a cup of warm milk. It helps her sleep better.

Dylan holds his toy dog.
He sleeps with it every night.

Kaylee listens to
music before bedtime.

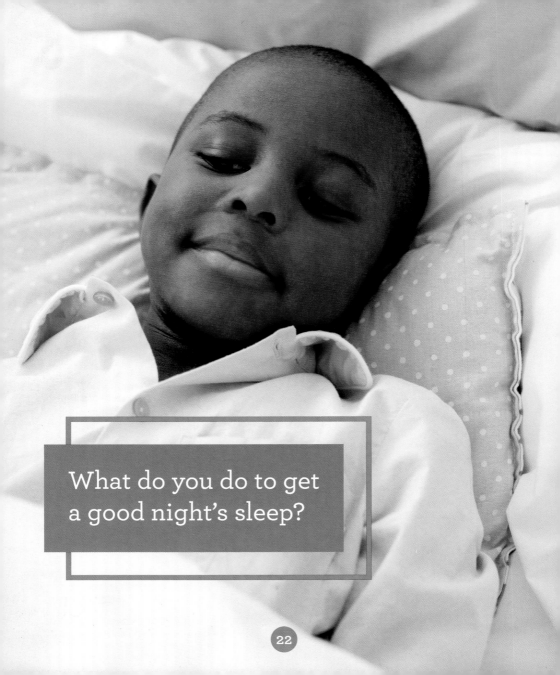

What do you do to get a good night's sleep?

HEALTH QUIZ

1. It is easy to pay **attention** in school if you are tired. True or False?

2. You can feel too tired to play if you don't get enough sleep. True or False?

3. Morgan drinks a cup of warm milk. True or False?

4. Dylan sleeps with his toy elephant. True or False?

5. Kaylee listens to music before bedtime. True or False?

Answers: 1. False 2. True 3. True 4. False 5. True

GLOSSARY

asleep – in a state of sleep, or not awake.

attention – the act of concentrating on or giving careful thought to something.

habit – a behavior done so often that it becomes automatic.